THE COLLECTORS

Selected Works by Philip Pullman

THE COLLECTORS

Philip Pullman

Illustrations by Tom Duxbury

PENGUIN BOOKS

PENGUIN BOOKS

UK | USA | Canada | Ireland | Australia
India | New Zealand | South Africa

Penguin Books is part of the Penguin Random House group of companies
whose addresses can be found at global.penguinrandomhouse.com.

www.penguin.co.uk   www.puffin.co.uk   www.ladybird.co.uk

Penguin
Random House
UK

First published in Great Britain as an audio story by Audible 2014
Published as a digital edition by RHCP Digital 2015
This hardback edition published 2022

001

Text design by Janene Spencer

Typeset in 12/17 Baskerville MT Pro
Printed in Great Britain by Clays Ltd, Elcograf S.p.A.

A CIP catalogue record for this book is available from the British Library

ISBN: 978–0–241–47525–6

All correspondence to:
Penguin Books
Penguin Random House Children's
One Embassy Gardens, 8 Viaduct Gardens, London SW11 7BW

This story is dedicated with thanks and admiration to Kate Bush, who told me the original a long time ago.

'But the *thing is*,' said Horley, 'they didn't know each other at all. Never heard of each other. It wasn't about the makers. Only about the works.'

'And how did you hear about it?' said Grinstead.

'From the dealer who sold me the painting. Falcondale. Max Falcondale.'

'Reliable?'

'Well, within limits, you know, but he'd made the sale anyway. He just wanted to tell the story.'

It was the December of 1970, and they were sitting in the Senior Common Room of Horley's college after dinner. It was cold, and the dinner had been meagre and dull, culminating in some sort of nut pudding that

closely resembled wet cement. The small fire in the SCR had just enough energy to warm the rug directly in front of it, and left the corners of the room to fend for themselves. There was more warmth coming from the two

standard lamps on either side of the hearth. The company wasn't large: the Librarian, the Chaplain, a couple of young Fellows no one seemed to know by name, a visiting professor of philology, and Grinstead, Horley's guest for the evening. While the rest discussed European politics, Horley and Grinstead, occupying the shadows at the end of a sofa and the deepest armchair respectively, spoke quietly about a painting in Horley's possession.

Grinstead sipped his brandy and said quietly, 'Well, tell me what Falcondale said.'

'He told me the story as he'd heard it from the painter's daughter. Leonora Skipton. Her father usually painted landscapes in a sort of second-hand Impressionist manner, nothing especially original, but agreeable enough. He very rarely did portraits. This one was quite out of his usual range. Falcondale had no idea who the sitter was – a fair-haired young woman with the most extraordinarily ambiguous expression – one moment she looks cold, disdainful, contemptuous even, and the next on fire with a sort of lost and hopeless and yet somehow very sexy yearning. A very *strong* picture.'

'What's she doing?'

'She's standing in front of a sort of dusty pink curtain, hands clasped in front, wearing a simple dark blue blouse thing and a cream-coloured skirt. Very plain, very simple. It's all in the face.'

'She wasn't the daughter – Leonora, was it?' said Grinstead.

'No. The daughter couldn't stand the picture – loathed it. She came in to Falcondale's

gallery to confirm the identification, and said she wished it had been burnt the day it was painted. That was all she'd say. She's some incredible age – must be nearly a hundred. Oh, and he showed me a remarkable letter—'

'And what about the other piece?'

'Ah. A little bronze, about a foot high. French, sort of Symbolist, I suppose you'd call it. A monkey, or an ape, I never remember the difference, sitting up with one hand reaching out towards us, or, you know, towards some fruit or something. The expression's the thing here too. Absolute savage greed and brutality. Horrible thing to look at – I don't know how anyone could bear to have it around. But beautifully sculpted, you know, every hair, every little fingernail in place, perfect. And in the body a tension, an energy – any second it might spring at you and tear your eyes out . . . Ghastly thing, really. But brilliantly sculpted.'

'And who made that?'

'Marc-Antoine Duparc. Ever heard of him?'

'Yes, actually. Minor Symbolist, as you say. Was it a large edition, this bronze? Lot of them about?'

'I'd be surprised if there were any others. There's just this particular one.'

'Has it got a tail?'

'Yes, I think it has. Curled around its feet.'

'Then it's a monkey.'

'Oh, is that the difference? Well, a monkey then.'

The visiting professor of philology laboured to his feet, swaying slightly.

'Goodnight, gentlemen,' he said. 'A highly enjoyable evening. I am most grateful. If someone could be kind enough – I forget where it is, my room – I would be so thankful for a guide, or at least an indication of the direction . . .'

He nearly lost his balance for a moment and put his hand to the mantelpiece to regain it. One of the young Fellows sprang up and offered to help.

The Chaplain got up to shake the professor's hand, the Librarian followed his example, and it took at least two minutes to get the old man out of the Senior Common Room and into his overcoat and away. The Librarian looked back at the fire.

'Is it worth another log, d'you think?' he said, though he plainly thought it would be an intolerable expense.

'Those logs are juniper, I believe?' said Grinstead.

'They are, sir, the last of a large consignment from the college's forest land in Wales. Land now sold, I'm very sorry to say.'

No one spoke. The Librarian sighed almost silently, and lifted the smallest log out of the basket and placed it at the edge of the fire.

'Well, I must make sure the professor has

found his rooms,' he said. 'Goodnight, gentlemen.' He left, and a silence fell in the room.

'I too should go,' said the aged Chaplain after a pause. 'I think I shall be on my way. Goodnight, Horley. Goodnight, sir,' he said to Grinstead; 'goodnight, er . . . h'mm,' he added to the remaining Fellow, who stood up to shake hands before nodding a goodnight to Horley and Grinstead, and following the old man out.

Horley went to place the Librarian's log more centrally on the fire, and added another from the basket before taking the armchair under the standard lamp next to the hearth.

'Come over this way,' he said. 'Damned cold away from the fire. That was typical, Bolton's reluctance to burn another log. This college is riddled with parsimony. D'you realise that the phone system is so old that if the porter's not physically present at the actual switchboard, none of us can phone out?'

'Extraordinary,' said Grinstead.

He came to sit on the sofa opposite, and cast a glance around the dark-panelled walls at the five or six portraits of previous Principals or benefactors.

'Not up to much, are they?' said Horley. 'The Millais drawing of Principal Ledger isn't bad, but the rest . . .' He gave a dismissive wave.

'You were telling me about the bronze monkey,' said Grinstead.

'Monkey. Yes. Well, in itself it wasn't – isn't – worth very much. A curiosity, really. You'd need to have peculiar tastes to want the thing

'Why did *you* buy it?'

'Ah, you see, I didn't. Now we come to the mystery. It seems that by chance, purely by chance, the bronze and the painting often ended up in the same collections. Someone would buy the painting, and a few months later the bronze would come up for auction, and they'd buy that. Or the other way round. Or they'd buy the one and then be given the other as a gift, or win it in a bet, or something. Without anyone intending it, the painting and the bronze would find themselves in the same room, time and time again. Falcondale was the first to notice it. He told me about it, and I was sceptical, of course, but he had the records. He'd followed it right back. I had to admit, there was something going on.'

'So who bought the monkey last?'

'A man who owed me some money. Bought a Charpentier mezzotint from me and never paid. Lawyer chased him up, and he offered the monkey instead. In Bonnier's valuation, it was worth a fair bit more than he owed me, so I took it. I had no idea of the connection then. It was only last week, when I bought the painting, that Falcondale began to open up.'

'You're sure he wasn't making it up?'

'Pretty sure. The business was going on before he was born. Before any of us were born.'

'You were going to say something about a letter.'

'Oh yes. Falcondale had a letter – he gave me a copy of it – from a woman in Moscow to a distant cousin in London.

A minor aristocrat of some sort. Written in French, about seventy years ago, before the revolution, anyway, about a scandal in her social circle. The husband of a friend of hers was a diplomat, and he'd been representing Russia at some high-level talks in Paris, and somebody had shown him the monkey and he rather fancied it. So he made an offer and they accepted it, and the bronze went home to Moscow in his baggage. As soon as his wife saw it, she hated it and wanted it out of the house. She thought it was an embodiment of pure evil. But the husband dug his heels in and refused to get rid of it, so the wife consulted her priest, who tried to exorcise it. He spent the night in the salon where the husband kept the thing, praying and, you know, whatever they do, and when the wife came down in the morning, there was the priest dead on the floor, head bashed in, and the monkey on the sideboard, covered in blood.'

'Good God,' said Grinstead. 'Who did it?'

'They never found out. Husband was badly shaken, of course, and when the police took it away as evidence, he never asked for it back. They couldn't find anyone to charge, so after a year or so they put it up for auction, and it was bought by a collector who gave it pretty sharpish to a Moscow gallery where it found itself in the same room as the painting. Again.'

Grinstead drank the last of his brandy. 'And now it's yours,' he said. 'They're both yours.'

'Yes, both mine.'

'Are you going to keep them?'

'I thought what I'd do,' said Horley, 'just to be mischievous, is adjust my will and leave the painting to this college and the monkey to Merton.'

There was an ancient rivalry between Merton and Horley's college.

Grinstead nodded. 'Sound plan,' he said. 'Are you going to show me these things?'

'Oh, would you like to see them?' said Horley in mock-surprise. 'I haven't even unpacked the monkey yet. It arrived this morning.'

'Well, let's go and do that,' said Grinstead. 'This room's getting colder and colder.'

* * *

A fine freezing rain was drifting down into the quad as they left for Horley's rooms. There were only two windows lit in the old buildings, and as Grinstead looked around, one of those went out.

'Who was this chap who owed you money for the mezzotint?' Grinstead said.

'Rainsford. I was never sure I could trust him. D'you know him?'

'I bought a drawing from him once. A Vernet. It was a fake.'

They climbed the stairs to Horley's rooms. The light was on a timer switch, and by the time Horley was fumbling with his keys, the light went out.

'More penny-pinching,' he said. 'What would it cost them to give us an extra thirty seconds of light? Anyway –' he opened the door, and stood back – 'welcome to the warmest room in the building.'

'My God, it is too,' said Grinstead.

It was suffocating. It was actually hot. The fire was burning fiercely, the heavy curtains were drawn tight against draughts, and an electric fire with all three bars glowing red gave off an odour of toasted dust. Grinstead took off his overcoat at once.

Horley was bustling around, hanging up his gown, throwing his keys on the desk, taking out some wine glasses, clearing some books off the table next to the sofa, switching on a lamp.

'Perhaps we could economise a *little*,' he said, and switched off one bar of the electric fire.

'I'm certainly warm enough. Is this how you live, Horley, at this Turkish-bath temperature?'

'Only out of mischief. I like imagining the Bursar's expression as he sees the utility bills. Claret?'

'Go on then. Not a large glass. Where's this picture?'

'All in good time,' said Horley, sounding almost skittish.

Grinstead sat as far away from the fire as he could get, and took the glass Horley handed him. The wine was sour and unpleasant, but so was the wine they'd had at dinner.

'D'you remember the first picture you bought?' said Grinstead.

Horley was adjusting the angle of the lampshade so as to shine clearly on the desk opposite. 'Yes, I do,' he said. 'It was a dirty postcard. I bought it in Egypt during my

national service. I kept it for a week, and then I felt rather ashamed and threw it away. I mean, the composition was *lamentable*. Never looked back, really.'

'Start of a great career.'

'Well, here she is, that not impossible she, whatever her name is . . .'

The picture was resting on a little easel on the desk, a small thing, no more than fifteen inches tall and twelve across. Horley removed a black velvet cloth with a silly flourish that Grinstead completely ignored. The painting, oil on canvas in a pretty gilt frame, glowed in the lamplight as if there was a bloom on the colours. The young woman stood modestly, hands entwined, head slightly tilted, fair curly hair loosely restrained behind her neck with a red ribbon. Grinstead's eyes were fixed on the face in the picture, and Horley was taken aback by the intensity of the visitor's gaze, until he remembered that the man was a collector, after all. But this was more than acquisitive connoisseurship: it was feral. Grinstead's jaw was working – Horley could see the muscles tightening – and his lips were drawn back so that his clenched teeth were bared.

'D'you – er – have you seen her before?' Horley said.

'Yes. I know who she is.'

'Good Lord. How d'you know that?'

'We were lovers.'

'Oh, come on,' said Horley. 'What's her name then?'

'Marisa van Zee.'

Grinstead's eyes had not left the young

woman's face. As Horley followed the other man's gaze, the painted expression seemed to be showing another of its characteristic shifts of meaning: there was a little curve of happy triumph somewhere in the lines of the model's mouth and her eyes, though he found it impossible to see precisely where.

'But, Grinstead, this painting is seventy years old – probably nearer eighty! You're not being serious – I mean . . . What do you *mean*?'

'I mean that I knew her, and that for a short time we were lovers. She was the most remarkable woman I shall ever know.'

'What, *later* than this, when she was old? Is that what you mean? Oh, come on, man! For God's sake, I know we've drunk a fair amount—'

'It wasn't fair at all. It was disgusting, Horley. I don't know why you don't pour the whole cellar into the gutter and start again. Who's your wine chap?'

'Lepson – but . . .'

Horley lowered his jaw and blinked hard, as if trying to widen his eyes. He slipped his hand inside his jacket and scratched hard.

'What's the matter?' said Grinstead.

'Itching. Driving me mad.'

Horley had been trying not to scratch for some minutes now, but he couldn't hold off any more. He blinked again. He was conscious of not being as conscious as he would like to be.

'Sorry, Grinstead,' he said. 'I'm . . . I don't know what to say.'

'Never mind. Don't say anything. I've known this picture for half my life; I'm most grateful to you, Horley, I am really.'

'You *knew* about it, then?'

'I saw Skipton painting it.'

'And the monkey, and so on?'

'Yes, I knew that story. I've heard it a dozen times, and all incorrectly. I met Marisa van Zee in Skipton's studio when she was eighteen

and I was about five years older. I recognised something about her that you could never imagine.'

'What was that?'

'She came from another world.'

The electric fire gave a click as the switched-off bar reluctantly adjusted to its new temperature.

The soft roaring and popping of the fire was the only other sound, though Horley thought he could hear his own heart beating. The itching was growing intolerable.

'You're being metaphorical, of course,' he said. 'About knowing her, and so on. I mean, you know, eighty years – you must be about my age, and I'm not . . . I'm afraid I'm not following you at all. What did you say? Another world?'

'There are many worlds, Horley, many universes, an infinity of them, and none of them knows about any of the others. Except that at very rare intervals, a breach appears between one world and another. A little crack. Things slip through. Once you become attuned to it, you can spot things that don't come from here. There's a different sort of light that seems to play on them. That little pottery elephant on the shelf over there – I suppose you were told that was Assyrian, were you?'

'As a matter of fact, yes.'

'Well, it's not. It comes from another world. I couldn't tell you which one, I can just see that it does.'

'I see . . .' Horley said. 'And you met the young woman because of Skipton?' he went on carefully. He was feeling short of breath, as if he'd been running.

'Because I was working for old Garnier. Bertrand, the dealer, not his brother François. I had to call on Skipton about some small matter, and there she was. Instantaneous. I knew she was from another world, and she knew that I knew it.'

'Another world . . . Yes, of course. How had she come here, to this world? On a flying saucer?'

Grinstead looked at him, and Horley flinched.

'I'm being serious,' Grinstead said. 'Don't push it.'

'No, no . . . I'm not, really I'm not. I'm – I'm – I'm – I just – it's – it's all *unfamiliar*, you must see that?'

'Yes, I do see that. Perfectly reasonable point. Well, in theory all these worlds are mutually unreachable. The physics wouldn't allow things to be otherwise. In practice, the whole structure . . . leaks. Things get picked up and put down on a window sill, for example, that opens just once, just briefly, into another world; someone passing by takes a fancy to it, and off it goes, never to be seen again. Your little pottery elephant, Marisa van Zee, here a blackbird, there a bus timetable . . . A small ɔy has an imaginary friend – they play together for hours – whisper secrets, swear eternal love, play at being king and queen . . . But she's not imaginary, she comes through that tumbled bit of wall behind the greenhouse, and one day he finds that someone's mended it, and she's lost for ever. Or that house you saw from the train window, that little glimpse of the perfect dwelling, and you make the same journey over and over and you never see it again. Well, that's what's happening: an infinity of worlds, and a thousand and one little leaks in the fabric.'

'And these other worlds – are they all the same as this one?'

'No. Some of them are just like this one, except for one detail. Imagine a world just like this, for example, but where every human

being has an animal spirit accompanying them. A sort of visual spirit guide, animal totem, that sort of thing. Part of their own selves, but separate. For example.'

Horley looked at the picture, and then mopped his brow. 'I'm not sure that I can. Imagine it. How long did you . . . ?'

'How long did we have together? Less than a month. There were things she didn't want to tell me. I had an impression of high politics, of important negotiations, diplomatic secrets, but I respected her discretion. Meanwhile Skipton was painting this . . .'

Horley was scratching again, and breathing hard.

'But, Grinstead,' he said, 'this was eighty years ago, and you're not even fifty. I still can't get a sense of where you're sort of *standing* in all this. Are you talking about yourself, or about someone else? Is this fiction?'

'It's true. It happened to me. Time passes differently in different worlds. It might be eighty years ago in one perspective, but things don't always line up neatly.'

'So –' Horley was waving a hand loosely in the air, as if trying to catch a drifting mote of dust – 'so you and – and Marisa came from the same world?'

'That's not what I said.'

'No, course not. Grinstead, what . . .' Horley was trying to remember how this evening had come about. He must have invited Grinstead, since they were sitting in his college; but how did he know the man in the first place? It had completely slipped his mind. 'I think I must be drunk,' he said with great clarity.

'You were going to unpack the monkey.'

'Oh God, yes, the monkey . . . Better get the little brute out of his box. Stay there.'

Horley, tottering slightly, pulled a wooden box out from under the desk. It was formidably fastened with nails and heavy metal tape.

'Those nails are rusty,' said Grinstead. 'Be careful how you take them out.'

Horley was rummaging in a drawer behind his desk.

'Here we are,' he said, and held up a pair of pliers.

'You need something better than that. A proper nail-pull—'

'No, these are fine. Opened dozens of boxes.'

He worked the nose of the pliers under the metal tape, slipping several times, and tried to lever it up, without success. Then he attacked a nail head, without managing to grip it once.

'Screwdriver,' he said. 'In the drawer, Grinstead – would you mind?'

Grinstead put his glass down on the floor and went to look in the drawer. There was one screwdriver, whose head was worn and rounded. Horley took it and jammed it hard under the tape, levering upwards so hard that the blade of the screwdriver bent. Grinstead sat back down to watch. Horley next tried to stab the blade of the screwdriver under the lid,

and missed several times, but finally managed to lever it up. The wood splintered, but only at that spot. Horley stood up to take off his jacket. He was sweating, and there seemed to be a rash on his face. He was wheezing.

'Hammer,' he said. 'That's what we need.'

'Are you going to smash it entirely?'

'No, no, lever the – you know, the nail heads, with the claw. Lever them up. Don't know why I didn't think of it before.'

There was a hammer in the drawer. Horley blew out his cheeks and set to with the claw, and after great effort managed to lever one of the nails halfway out. Grinstead watched him closely.

'See! Just persistence. That's all you need,' Horley said.

'Of course.'

'Do it all now.'

'You're nearly there.'

'Absolutely.'

He continued bashing, levering, pulling, and finally managed to twist the metal tapes aside and over the edge of the top. He stood up, panting. His breath was wheezing in his throat.

'Grinstead, would you mind finishing it off?' he said. 'I'm not sure I . . .'

Grinstead took the hammer and pulled out the rest of the nails. It only took a minute. He lifted the top off the box and set it aside, and then reached down into the mass of crumpled paper and curls of wood shaving in which the bronze was packed.

'Here it is,' he said.

He lifted it out and unwrapped the final layer of tissue paper before setting the monkey on the desk next to the picture. It was just as repulsive as he remembered. He turned to Horley, who was gazing at it with an expression of horror.

'Horley? Surely you knew what it looked . . .'

'No, it's not . . .' Horley said, and swayed, clutching at the desk. The picture rocked on its easel. 'Grinstead – I'm not feeling very well – oh God . . .'

He stumbled towards the bedroom and flung open the door just in time to vomit into the washbasin inside it. His breathing was louder, high-pitched, and more laboured. It sounded like a very bad attack of asthma.

Grinstead stood up and looked at his watch.

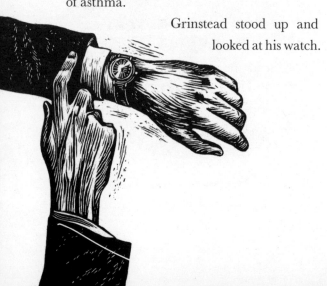

It was getting on for one o'clock. 'Horley? You all right?'

Horley's breath was rattling. 'Can't breathe,' he managed to say.

'Let me phone for an ambulance. You don't sound at all good.'

'No – can't phone out from here after midnight – the porter's off duty . . . Oh God—'

He was sick again.

'Go to the lodge,' he mumbled. 'Phone there somewhere – Grinstead, I'm frightened . . .'

'I'll be as quick as I can.'

Grinstead pressed the switch on the landing. The light went out before he reached the foot of the staircase. He stood inside the doorway and lit a cigarette. The rain had stopped falling, but the moisture in the air was gathering into a dense fog into which the buildings seemed to be dissolving; beyond the dark chapel roof, the air was saturated with a soft orange glow from the street outside. A distant mechanism began to whir quietly, and the chapel bell struck once.

Grinstead smoked the rest of the cigarette and went back upstairs. He held his breath and looked into the bedroom. Horley was dead. He pulled the door shut and turned back.

He looked around for something to carry the picture in, and saw Horley's briefcase, crammed with books and papers, lying on its side under the desk. Grinstead tipped everything out on the floor and found that

with a little persuasion the picture just fitted; it would have been a pity to cut it out of the frame, which was pretty, and suited it very well.

Then he took a pencil from the desk and moved the bunch of keys around until he saw

the one Horley had used to open the garden
door when he let them into the college earlier
on. Using a handkerchief to keep his
fingerprints off the rest of the bunch,
he detached the garden key and
put it in his pocket.

He looked around. There was nothing to suggest foul play, because after all there hadn't been any foul play. Two men had come here to have a drink and look at the bronze sculpture that had obviously been in the box (Grinstead picked up a shaving of wood and dropped it on the monkey's lap), the guest had left, the other had been overcome with some kind of food poisoning, and, unable to phone for help, died in his bedroom.

He left very quietly, carrying the briefcase. There was no need to take the monkey: it would follow in its own time. He found his way through the quad, into the garden and out of the door. He locked it again after him, and set off for his hotel through the freezing fog.

As he turned into the High Street, a taxi came along, too fast, and hit him. In his dark overcoat he was practically invisible, and he should have stopped to make sure the road was clear, but the taxi driver should have been going more slowly, with visibility so limited. The court found later that they were both to blame. The briefcase flew out of Grinstead's hand and landed on the pavement a moment after his head hit the road. He died at once.

* * *

'Anaphylactic shock,' said the Bursar to the Chaplain as they stood in Horley's rooms some days later.

'What's that?'

'When you eat something you're allergic to. Nuts, quite often. That's what did him in, apparently.'

'Didn't we have that rather nice nut pudding of Chef's that night?'

'Don't know. I wasn't dining that night. I wonder if . . . Well, it's too late to make any difference now.'

'But wouldn't he have known, if he was allergic to nuts?'

'Apparently sometimes not. You find out when the thing kicks in, which it might do at once or it might take a couple of hours, and then you've only got a few minutes.'

'Poor man,' said the Chaplain. 'I expect his guest would have gone by that time.'

The Bursar cast a sideways glance at his colleague, who was gazing sorrowfully at the bronze monkey. 'That's what we must suppose,' he said.

'And what about his possessions? He's got an awful lot of pictures and things.'

'We'll have to make an inventory. He seems to have had no family except an unmarried

sister, and I have no idea if he left a will. There's a lot of work involved.'

'And what are you carrying, Charles? What's in that parcel? Something of his?'

'Well,' said the Bursar. 'It's rather odd. On the same night, it seems that a chap was

knocked down in the High – you remember how foggy it was?'

'Yes, I do. Beastly.'

'That chap was Horley's guest. Had been Horley's guest, I suppose one should say. Killed at once.'

'No! Both died on the same night?'

'And he seems to have been carrying Horley's briefcase, containing this painting.' He took the picture out of the brown-paper parcel and set it on the little easel, next to the monkey. 'So what d'you make of that, Eric?'

The Chaplain's old pale blue eyes were wide. 'Extraordinary! D'you think Horley had just given him the painting? Or perhaps sold it to him? What a tragic business!'

'If he'd sold it, there'd be a receipt or something of the sort, but we haven't found

one. Since there's no evidence it belonged to the other chap, we have to assume it was Horley's. We'll count it all up in the inventory.'

'What a very pretty girl. D'you know who she is?'

'No idea,' said the Bursar, 'but she looks mighty pleased with herself.'

Philip Pullman was born in Norwich and educated in England, Zimbabwe, Australia and Wales. He studied English at Exeter College, Oxford.

His first children's book, *Count Karlstein*, was published in 1982. To date, he has published thirty-three books, read by children and adults alike. His most famous work is the *His Dark Materials* trilogy. These books have been honoured by several prizes, including the Carnegie Medal, the Guardian Children's Book Prize, and (for *The Amber Spyglass*) the Whitbread Book of the Year Award – the first time that prize had been given to a children's book. Pullman has received numerous other awards, including the Eleanor Farjeon Award and the Astrid Lindgren Award. He was knighted in the 2019 New Year's Honours List for services to literature.

Tom Duxbury is an illustrator from the moors of West Yorkshire. His work is influenced by lino-printing, which he uses to depict feeling, movement and nostalgia. He is inspired by the spirit of nature and the narrative of a landscape.